MOUNTAIN BIKING
...to the Extreme:

Cliff Dive

YOUTH FICTION
BY SIGMUND BROUWER

Short Cut Series
#1 *Snowboarding . . . to the Extreme: Rippin'*
#2 *Mountain Biking . . . to the Extreme: Cliff Dive*
#3 *Skydiving . . . to the Extreme: 'Chute Roll*
#4 *Scuba Diving . . . to the Extreme: Off the Wall*

Lightning on Ice Series
#1 *Rebel Glory*
#2 *All-Star Pride*
#3 *Thunderbird Spirit*
#4 *Winter Hawk Star*
#5 *Blazer Drive*
#6 *Chief Honor*

The Accidental Detectives Mystery Series

Winds of Light Medieval Adventures

SHORT CUTS
SERIES™

MOUNTAIN BIKING
... to the Extreme:

Cliff Dive

Sigmund Brouwer

WORD kids!

WORD PUBLISHING
Dallas·London·Vancouver·Melbourne

Mountain Biking . . . to the Extreme: Cliff Dive

Copyright © 1996 by Sigmund Brouwer.

Managing Editor: Laura Minchew
Project Editor: Beverly Phillips

Library of Congress Cataloging-in-Publication Data

Brouwer, Sigmund, 1959–
    Mountain Biking—to the extreme—cliff dive /
    Sigmund Brouwer.
    p. cm. — (Short cuts ; 2)
    Summary: While training for a mountain bike race
in his Texan border town, fifteen-year-old Blake comes
into possession of a backpack of hundred-dollar
bills—an event that just might kill him.
    ISBN 0-8499-3952-6 (trade paper)
    [1. Mystery and detective stories. 2. Criminals—
Fiction. 3. All terrain cycling—Fiction.] I. Title.
II. Series. III. Series: Brouwer, Sigmund, 1959–
Short cuts ; 2.
PZ7.B79984Mo   1996
[Fic]—dc20

96-24551
CIP
AC

Printed in the United States of America

00 OPM 9 8 7 6

To
Intermountain Christian School,
and especially to the 1995–96 7th-grade
class for their help with this book:

*Libby, Tyler, Noah, Melisa, Brew,
Jeremy, Nick, Katie, Laura, Chris,
Troy, Jon, Ann, Charitee, Matt, Rachel,
Brooke, Forrest, Joanna, Michael,
Adam, Jordan, Seth, Brett, Whitney,
Than, Jordan, and Amy.*

Chapter One

Yahoo!" I shouted into the wind. Sometimes on my mountain bike, I have so much fun that I have to shout. This was one of those times. I was on a smooth path going straight downhill. The wind was in my face, and I felt like an eagle in a full dive.

"Yahoo!" I didn't have to worry about my friend Tommy hearing me. We were both practicing for the yearly Summit Race, the biggest sport event of the area. I had left Tommy way behind on the uphill climb. Going down I had such a big head start, it would take him a week to catch up. And that was only if I decided to stop. At the speed I was going now, he would be two weeks behind me by the time I reached the bottom.

The Summit Trail was a bike path through the desert hills outside of the town where I live. It has sections where it is packed smooth. Other spots have big boulders; others are sand. I had been over the trail so many times, I knew all of it.

Because of that, I was ready for the big hole up ahead. I turned my handlebars slightly and aimed to the right of the hole. That sent me over a patch of bumps. I half stood on my pedals and let my knees take the bounces.

There was a sharp corner after that. I squeezed my hand brakes. I squeezed just a little. I didn't want to slow down too much. The timer on my wristwatch was counting every second, and I thought I had a good chance at beating my own record.

I leaned into the turn, loving life.

"Ya—" I didn't get a chance to finish. Some idiot with a pack on his back stood beside his mountain bike. Right in the middle of the path!

I hit my brakes as hard as I could. I pulled

my weight back so I wouldn't fly over my handlebars.

The guy saw me coming and tried to pull his bike out of the way. But I could see I was going to hit him. I had to do something to avoid hitting him head-on and getting flipped off my bike.

I let go of my front brake and cranked hard to the left. At the same time, I leaned over, almost laying my bike flat. The back end skidded around. My back tire slapped into his front tire.

THUMP.

I dropped my bike and jumped clear.

"Hey," I said, "next time pull your bike to the side. You could get hurt parking smack in the middle of the trail."

"Shut up," he said.

I blinked in surprise. It was his fault I'd nearly hit him. If I hadn't made such a good move, both of us could have been hurt real bad. And he was telling me to shut up?

"Shut up?" I repeated.

"Shut up," he said again. He dropped his bike and picked mine up.

"Hey!" *First he tells me to shut up and then he grabs my bike?* "What are you doing?"

"What's it look like I'm doing?" he asked.

"Looks like you're taking my bike."

"Exactly," he said. "My bike has a flat."

"You can't take mine," I said.

He smiled a mean, ugly smile. He swung his leg to get on my bike. "Just try to stop me."

Chapter Two

I stepped toward him. He was a couple of inches taller than me and a whole bunch of pounds heavier. I'm tall, but skinny, mainly from all the bike riding I do. Still, I wasn't going to let him take my Exotec-4 mountain bike. I had saved for a year to buy it.

I grabbed my bike by the handlebars and pulled. "Let go," I told him.

Both of my hands were on my bike. That was a bad move. He punched at my face. Hard and fast. I couldn't bring my hands up fast enough to defend myself. His punch knocked me backward. I tripped over a rock and fell.

When I looked up, he was already on my bike and peddling away.

I jumped to my feet and dove forward. I managed to get my fingers around one of the straps of his backpack. His upper body spun toward me.

"It's my bike," I shouted. "Drop it!" I kept a bulldog grip on the strap.

He slipped one arm loose from the strap. Wearing just one strap, he twisted and punched me again.

"Hey!" I shouted. "Quit it!"

"Hey what?" someone shouted from behind us. It was Tommy. Tommy lifts weights. He's slow on his mountain bike because he blocks so much wind.

The guy on my bike saw Tommy. He must have decided that he would lose against us both. He tried to get away from me. I held on to his backpack, getting dragged along.

There was a ripping sound. The second strap of his pack tore lose. I went flying backward, and he went flying ahead.

I landed on my back with his backpack in my hands. He kept going down the hill, on my bike.

Tommy stopped beside me. "Your face, man. It's bleeding."

"My bike," I said. I managed to get up again. With one hand I held the backpack. With the other hand, I wiped my nose. It hurt. My teeth hurt. My face hurt. "He's got my bike."

"What are you talking about?" Tommy asked. "It's behind you on the ground. Why were you jumping that guy?"

"That's *his* bike on the ground. He's got mine. He stole it from me."

Tommy and I watched the guy on my bike. He was a long way down the hill already. There was no way we could catch him.

"Your bike?" Tommy said, like he couldn't believe it.

"My bike." I could hardly believe it myself, it had happened so fast.

We watched him turn off the Summit Trail and take another path, this one much narrower.

I looked at Tommy. Tommy looked at me. We had been everywhere in these hills on our bikes. We knew every single path. We both grinned. We knew the same thing about the path the guy just took.

"Well," Tommy said through his grin, "if he just stole your bike, it's a good thing he turned down a dead end."

He patted the seat of his bike.

"Hop on," he said. "Let's go get him."

Chapter Three

Once we reached the second path, we had to go slow. The path ran between big boulders and was not as wide as the Summit Trail.

It didn't matter that we had to go slow. This was rough desert country. The path down ran into a narrow canyon. The rock walls on both sides of the canyon were too steep to climb. Even if he ditched my bike and tried to run, the guy had only one place to go. Straight ahead.

The path became so narrow that I had to get off the bike. Tommy rode ahead slowly. I jogged behind him. As my feet pounded the ground, my nose hurt even more. I was getting tired of carrying the guy's backpack.

"Did he say anything?" Tommy asked.

"Just told me to shut up. Then he grabbed my bike. Then he punched me and took off."

"Have you ever seen him before?"

"Yes," I said. The guy had a really wide face. It made him look like a melon head. He was easy to remember. "I've seen him a couple of times. Always on the Summit Trail."

"Do you think he's training for the race?"

"No way," I said. "He always rides fast. But he's too old for the race."

The low mountains here were perfect for mountain bike racing. The Summit Race was a national event, and the town went crazy over it. Racers had to be sixteen or younger to enter. Melonhead looked old enough to be out of high school.

"Well," Tommy said, "you'll get your chance to talk to him pretty soon. Around the next corner is Devil's Leap. We both know what that means."

It meant the bike thief had no place to go. Devil's Leap is like a giant crack in the rock of the desert hills. It runs across the trail. It is wider than a bus is long. And it's so deep that if you drop a rock into it, it takes three seconds to hear the rock hit bottom. You can only do one thing when you reach Devil's Leap: turn around.

My heart started beating even faster. I was glad that Tommy was with me. The melon-headed guy had a mean swing. I didn't want to be his punching bag again.

We rounded the corner.

"What?!" Tommy yelled.

The guy was nowhere in sight.

The trail led to the edge of Devil's Leap. There was another bike trail that dead-ended on the other side of Devil's Leap. In between was nothing but air. And the straight drop far, far to the bottom of Devil's Leap.

"I don't get it," I said. "The guy must have wings."

"I don't get it either." Tommy pointed at the steep cliff walls around us. "No one could climb those. Especially carrying your bike."

I dropped the guy's backpack on the ground. I slowly walked closer to the edge. "Maybe he came around the corner too fast," I said. "Maybe he didn't know about the drop-off. Maybe he didn't stop in time."

I could hardly stand to look over the edge. I'm scared of heights, real scared. Way, way down were more boulders. The bottom of Devil's Leap filled with water during flash floods. When it was dry, it was just sand and rock. During a rainstorm, though, water moved through it like a freight train.

I checked to see if there was a body down there. My palms began to sweat as I looked down. I couldn't imagine how bad it would be to take a cliff dive here.

"I don't see anything down there," I said. "Any ideas, Tommy?"

Tommy didn't say anything.

"Tommy?" I said again.

He still didn't say anything.

I was so close to the edge that I didn't dare turn around. I didn't want to lose my balance and fall. Instead, I backed away from the edge. When I felt safe, I turned my head to look at Tommy.

And I saw why he had not heard me.

The backpack was at his feet. And spilling from the backpack were bundles of money.

I ran close to get a better look.

They were bundles of hundred-dollar bills.

"We're rich," Tommy said. He held a bundle of money in each hand. "We're rich enough to retire, and we haven't even graduated from high school yet."

Chapter Four

You want to do what?" Tommy said. We were on the main highway into town. He rode his bike. I rode the bike that the melon-headed guy had left behind. Tommy and I had fixed the flat tire with Tommy's repair kit. That made more sense than walking all the way back.

As we rode, we didn't have to worry about traffic. We live in a small town. The highway and streets are very quiet.

"I want to turn the money over to the police," I said. I had been thinking about it ever since we left Devil's Leap. It had taken us an hour to get this far.

"Are you crazy?" he asked.

"It would be more nuts to keep the money," I said. I looked at Tommy, but I could hardly see his face. It was almost dark outside. My parents wouldn't be worried though. I usually rode for hours after school.

"Nuts to keep the money?" he echoed. "You turn sixteen next month. Would it be nuts to drive a brand-new Corvette when you get your license?"

"And you turn sixteen the month after that," I said. "Wouldn't you like to reach your sixteenth birthday?"

"What do you mean?"

"Tell me," I said, "where do we live?"

Tommy rolled his eyeballs. "Now I know you've lost your mind. You can't even remember where we live."

"Nowhere, Texas," I said. "On the American side of the Rio Grande."

"What's the river got to do with it?"

"Mexico is on the other side of the river," I told him.

"You're still not telling me why we should turn the money in," he said.

"We live in a border town. People smuggle things in and out of border towns. You know. Like drugs."

"So? We're rich. What do drugs have to do with the backpack full of money?"

"What if this money comes from drug dealing?" I asked. "I mean, regular business people don't carry huge bundles of cash around in a backpack."

He shrugged.

"Tommy," I said. "That money belongs to someone. There might be close to a million dollars in the backpack. Don't you think someone might come looking for it? Don't you think someone will do almost anything to get it back?"

"You're right," he said. "So how about we just keep it a secret between you and me?"

"I don't think that would be smart," I said, "The melon-headed guy saw me. And people who deal drugs can be real nasty. They're not afraid to break the law. You know, like laws against murdering two teenage kids who have their money."

"Fine," he said. "You go ahead and give the money to the police. But you do it by yourself."

"Huh?" I said. We had entered the town. There were service stations and restaurants at the edge. Beyond that was the quiet neighborhood where Tommy and I lived.

"Turn it in by yourself," he said again. He stopped his mountain bike. I stopped beside him. He looked me straight in the eyes. "And don't tell them I was with you."

"Why not?"

"For starts," Tommy said, "my dad. You know he wants me to be the perfect student. He'll go crazy if he thinks I was involved with drug money. And no matter how I explain it, he'll think I did something wrong."

"All right," I said. "I guess I don't have to let the police know you were with me."

"And there's another reason," he said. "I don't want people to know I was stupid enough to give away all that money."

Tommy rode away without looking back. He left me in the dust, holding a backpack with a million dollars.

For a couple of minutes, I was tempted to keep it. I thought of my dad. He fixed cars for a living, and I was proud of what people thought of him. Everyone around knew he was honest and hard working. That respect was worth much more than money.

I knew what my dad would want me to do. I told myself I would turn the money in to the sheriff.

Then I was tempted to take just enough to buy myself a new mountain bike. The melon-headed guy's bike wasn't nearly as nice as mine. My Exotec-4 had twenty-one gears, with the gear shifts on the handle-bars. It had shocks on the front wheel. I wanted my bike, not his. It would be right, I told myself, to keep just enough money to get a new bike.

I thought about it awhile longer. I couldn't fool myself. Stealing money was stealing money, whether I stole a lot or a little. I wanted to be able to look my dad in the eye without feeling like a thief.

I thought of something else. Whoever the money belonged to probably knew how much was there. If any was missing, they would know. Drug dealers could be just as nasty over a little money missing as over a lot of money missing.

I rode toward the police station. All the way there, I expected a car full of bad guys to blast me with a machine gun. After all, people have died for a lot less than a million dollars.

Chapter Five

How are you doing, Blake?" Sheriff Charlie Werkle asked.

Because we lived in a small town, I had known Sheriff Werkle since I was a kid. Before he became sheriff, he had run a business with his brother Floyd. Now that Charlie was sheriff, Floyd ran Werkle's Printing & Engraving by himself. It was a business that printed or engraved anything from business cards to brochures to trophies. In fact, the huge trophies for the Summit Race were donated by Werkle's Printing & Engraving.

Sheriff Werkle was a tall man, nearly bald. He wore a brown uniform. There were dark circles of sweat around his armpits. His hat was on the counter beside him. He kept smiling as I walked up to the counter.

"I'm fine," I answered. "Except for this backpack full of money."

I opened it and set it on the counter between us. "See?"

He looked. He whistled. There was no one but me to hear him whistle. Sheriff Werkle is the only policeman in our town. His secretary had already left for the day. There was one jail cell in the office, and it was empty.

"Son, where did this come from?"

I told him everything that had happened. I told him I had been training for the big Summit Race. I told him about the guy with the melon head. I told him how my bike had been stolen.

"He just left you there with the backpack?"

"Yes," I said.

"Why didn't he keep fighting?" Sheriff Werkle wondered. "It seems strange that he would run off and leave you with all this money."

"Someone came by and scared him off," I answered. That part was true, of course. I hoped, though, the sheriff wouldn't ask me for more details. I had promised not to bring Tommy into this, but I didn't want to lie.

"Scared him off, huh?" Sheriff said. "Lucky for you."

I nodded yes. My nose and cheekbones still hurt from where the melon-headed guy had punched me.

"Well," Sheriff Werkle said. "Let's see how much is here."

He dumped the backpack over and whistled again. Bundle after bundle of hundred-dollar bills spread across the counter. I noticed all the bundles were crisp and new.

"We're going to have to put this in a safe," he said.

He frowned at me. "You didn't take any, did you?"

"No," I said. "I wanted to, but I didn't."

"Good," he said. "If no one claims this money, we'll see that you get it back."

"Really?" I hadn't thought of that. "Wow!"

Sheriff Werkle smiled. He put his finger to his lips and pretended to shush me. "You'll have to be quiet about this, though. Don't even tell anyone in your family."

"Why not?" I asked.

"Think about it," he said. "If word gets out about this money, everyone and their dog will try to claim it. We won't know who it belongs to. But if no one knows about the money, only the person who lost it will come looking for it."

"I get it," I said.

"Not only that," the sheriff added, "we'll only hand this money over if someone can tell us the exact amount."

He smiled at me. "See, I'll be doing my best to protect it. It will only go to the person who lost it. And if no one shows up in four weeks, you'll get the money. But only if you keep it a secret. Got that? Not even your mother and father. It will be much better to surprise them with the money when it's actually yours."

"Not even my mother and father," I said. Sure, Tommy knew about it, but he would keep it a secret too. We would share the money in four weeks. The sheriff was right. It would be better to surprise Mom and Dad. I was already dreaming how great it would be to start throwing money around for them.

Sheriff Werkle smiled again. "Don't be surprised if no one claims this money. Whoever it belongs to probably doesn't want to explain anything about it. At least, not to a sheriff."

"Plus," I said, "whoever comes in for it will have to admit he stole my bike."

Sheriff Werkle chuckled. "Can't get your mind off your bike, huh?"

"I'd almost trade this money to get it back." I grinned. "Almost."

Sheriff Werkle pointed at the backpack on the counter.

"We'll count this together," he said. "I'll sign a note saying how much is here. You can keep the note. With this much money, we need to be as honest as possible."

It took us fifteen minutes to count the money. First, we counted the hundreds in one bundle. There were a hundred bills. That was $10,000. We decided each bundle probably held the same. Otherwise it would have taken forever to count it all.

There were ninety-five bundles. That meant the backpack held $950,000. My guess had been right. Nearly a million dollars.

Sheriff Werkle wrote the amount on a piece of paper. He put the date on the paper and signed it. "There you are. You can call me every few days to see if someone has claimed the money."

I grinned. "Thanks."

I picked up the backpack by its bottom. Something fell out of an inside pocket. It clunked onto the counter.

"Hey," I said. "That looks like a remote control for a television."

Sheriff Werkle picked it up and turned it over in his hands. "It sure does. I'll throw it in the safe with the money."

I should have wondered about that remote control. I should have wondered about a lot of things. But I didn't. I was too busy dreaming about how I would spend the money once I got it back.

I whistled as I walked outside. Stupid me.

Chapter Six

Even though I hoped to be rich, I knew one thing about money. Even close to a half million dollars—my share—would not buy me first place in the Summit Race. The race was a month away. The only way I would win was by practicing hard.

The next day after school, I went back out to the hills. Sheriff Werkle had said I could keep the melon-headed guy's bike until I got mine back. If I ever got it back.

I didn't enjoy riding this bike as much as my own. My Exotec-4 is one of the lightest mountain bikes you can buy. It's balanced perfectly. And it can take a lot of abuse.

I need a bike that takes a lot of abuse. When I ride, I never miss a chance to jump. I always take the hard way. I never back down from a steep hill.

That's why I decided today I would practice on the Undertaker.

It is named the Undertaker for a good reason. The run is so hard that it is never used for official races. Too many people could get hurt on it. It's a big loop run about ten miles long. Most of it follows the ridges of the mountains.

It took me a half hour to ride from town to the start of the Undertaker. I was riding alone, which is sometimes a bad idea. But I wanted to practice hard. Few of my friends can keep up when I'm riding hard. I wanted the freedom to keep my own pace.

But I did think about safety. I had my helmet on. And I had my water bottle. In the hot desert air, I sweat by the gallon. The last thing I wanted was to get cramps or to pass out from the heat. Especially riding alone.

At the bottom of the Undertaker, I looked up into the reddish rocks of the hills. It would be a hard ride.

I took a final breath. I was ready.

Behind me, I heard the low roar of an engine.

I looked back. Hardly anyone uses this road. Maybe some other mountain bikers had come out for the challenge.

Coming toward me was a 4 x 4 truck. I couldn't see the driver. The windows were smoked glass and very dark. I recognized the truck from earlier in the day. Had it been following me?

The truck began to slow down.

I didn't like that.

I began to pedal up the Undertaker as fast as I could. Maybe I was being paranoid, but it seemed better to be safe than sorry.

The truck stopped.

I peeked backward.

A man jumped out of the driver's side.

I didn't like that at all. I recognized the melon-headed guy who had punched me and stolen my bike. Worse, he had a rifle slung over his shoulder.

I pedaled harder. Because of the tough path, I didn't get much of a head start.

The melon-headed guy didn't shout at me to stop. I didn't like that either. If he was after me, he wasn't worried that I might get away.

I heard the zing first, then the loud crack. It took me a second to figure it out. The zing had been a bullet, traveling faster than the speed of sound. The sound of the rifle shot had caught up to me a half second later.

I pedaled harder. Another fifty yards up the hill the trail disappeared behind some rocks.

Another bullet zinged.

I busted hard, zigging and zagging. I expected to be picked from my bike by a bullet—thrown to the ground like a piece of dead meat.

Somehow, I made it to the turn. Behind a huge boulder, I stopped. My lungs felt like I had been breathing fire. My legs were shaky.

I told myself to relax. I was safe. Melonhead couldn't see me up here in the rocks. If he couldn't see me, he couldn't shoot me.

I crawled along the ground and peeked around the boulder. If he was aiming to shoot me, he wouldn't expect my head to be that low.

What I saw terrified me.

He was unloading my mountain bike from the back of the truck.

Chapter Seven

I told myself not to panic. After all, mountain biking was my life. Because of that, it should be able to save my life. I had a big head start. I'd been training. I knew these trails. Melonhead wasn't going to get close enough to shoot at me again. At least, that's what I told myself.

I jumped on the bike I had been riding and headed up the Undertaker. I hoped I wouldn't *need* an undertaker before the day was over.

I reached a small dip in the trail. At the bottom, there was a narrow gully, filled with fist-sized rocks. I popped a wheelie and jumped the gully at full speed and landed pedaling hard.

After that, the trail rose again, steep and hard.

I pushed, glad for the twists and turns. Even if he got within a hundred yards, he wouldn't be able to see me. And if he did see me, it wouldn't be long before the trail turned again.

I climbed for a few minutes and reached a ridge.

Then came the downhill turn. Just as steep on the other side as the climb had been.

My "borrowed" bike screamed down the rock surface. I could feel the bike begin to slide out from under me. It was too dangerous to hit the brakes; I'd skid even more.

Instead, I dragged my right leg, desperate to slow down. I didn't see the small ramp of rocks until it was too late.

I hit the ramp at atomic speed. The bike flipped into the air. I held on tight. The bike landed on the back tire with the front tire turned just slightly. That popped me from the bike like a pea flung from a spoon. I thumped down on my left hip. The bike landed on top of me. The bike chain ripped across my shin.

I didn't have time to stop and worry about the blood.

I grabbed the bike and set it upright. The tire rims were straight. The chain was still together. I could ride.

And ride I did.

If I had been timing this run, I would have set a record.

Five minutes. Ten minutes. Fifteen minutes. I knew there was no way Melonhead was keeping up. He wasn't riding to save his life.

Then it happened. The trail turned upward again. I stood on the pedals to kick harder. And the chain snapped.

When I flipped earlier, the chain must have hit a rock. That could have weakened the master link. The master link is the small piece that holds the whole chain together.

What was I going to do?

Melonhead was somewhere behind me, getting closer every second. Worse, since this wasn't my bike, it didn't have a repair kit. How could I hold the chain together?

I figured the first thing I should do was to get me and the bike off the trail.

My leg stung where sweat mixed with the blood from the gash on my shin. I looked down. My sock was soaking up the blood. At least I didn't have to worry about him tracking me from a blood trail.

I grabbed the bike and threw it over my shoulder. There was a second, smaller path just behind me. A sign near it sent bikers back to the main trail.

A thought hit me as I ran toward the smaller trail. I stopped and yanked the sign out of the ground. Maybe if he didn't see the sign, he wouldn't even notice the second path.

I kept the sign in my hand and kept running with the bike over my shoulder. A few minutes later I stopped. I wanted to be close enough to the main trail to hear the melon-headed guy go past me.

I hid behind a big boulder and tried to get my breath back.

Ants started to crawl up my leg. I flicked them away.

Each minute seemed like an hour in the dentist chair. A guy with a rifle was after me.

And I was stuck with a bike that wouldn't move. Would he keep going when he got to the path? Or would he notice this path and come hunting me with his rifle?

Chapter Eight

A few minutes later, I heard him go by. I was safe, for now. But I still had to get back home. And the chain was still broken, dangling from the bike.

Then I noticed a small nail sticking out of the sign.

I grinned.

I pried the nail loose by pulling the sign apart.

I brought both ends of the chain together. I lined up the hole of the master link with the hole of the other link. I held my breath. Would the nail fit?

Yes!

The nail slid into the hole. Now that I knew it would fit, I pulled it out. I put it in from the other side, so the end of the nail faced toward me. The nail kept the two links from pulling apart. The chain was back together.

But I wasn't done.

I found a small rock and a big rock. I put the big rock behind the nail and chain. Using the small rock like a hammer, I pounded the nail to bend it. Now it wouldn't fall out or catch on anything.

It wasn't pretty, but it would work.

I got on the bike and pedaled back toward the Undertaker. The melon-headed guy still believed I was ahead of him. He would stay on the trail until it ended.

Me?

I went the other way. Back toward the beginning of the trail. Back toward the truck.

I went slowly. I didn't want to pop the nail loose from the chain. I didn't want to hurt myself again.

When I reached the truck, I wanted to keep going. But I knew if Melonhead got back in the next half hour, he could easily catch me.

So I let the air out of the front tires. And I pedaled away as fast as I dared.

Chapter Nine

Shot at you?" Sheriff Werkle asked. He stood up behind his desk. "Shot at you?"

"Yes, sir," I said. I told him about Melon-head and the rifle. And about the chase. I finished by telling him about the truck.

"I let the air out of the front tires," I said. "Maybe if you go out there, you can catch him."

Sheriff Werkle slammed his fist down on the counter. "He actually shot at you?!"

It made me feel better that he was so angry.

"I'm out the door," he said as he grabbed

his hat. "I'll see what I can do. Tell me again where you were riding."

I drew a small map.

"Thank you," he said. "I can promise you I'm going to do my best to stop him."

He paused halfway out the door. "No one has claimed the money, yet, Blake. If I can get this guy, we'll get the full story. There's a good chance you'll get to keep the money. Until then, keep this to yourself."

"Yes, sir," I said. "Can I call you later to find out if you got him?"

"You do that."

"Good luck," I said.

He frowned. He was still very angry. "He's the one who is going to need luck. You can count on that."

Chapter Ten

When I called Sheriff Werkle later, he told me that he hadn't found the truck. It made me a little scared, knowing that guy was still on the loose.

I think that's why I had the bad dream that night. In my dream, a guy with a giant head tried to bust into the house to get me. The dream was so real that I even heard the sound of breaking glass. Then I woke up. I *had* heard breaking glass.

I saw a crack of light beneath my bedroom door. Someone had turned on the hallway light.

I got out of bed, wearing my T-shirt and

boxers. I ran to the bedroom door and opened it. My dad was already at the end of the hallway. He had pulled on his pants but was shirtless. Mom was in the doorway of their bedroom, blinking at the light and rubbing her eyes.

"Dad?" I said.

"You heard it too?" he asked.

"Yes," I told him. "I heard it too."

Dad looks a lot like me. He's tall and thin. He has the same kind of sharp nose. We both have blond hair, but in opposite ways. He has five hairs on his head and the rest on his chest. Most of mine is on my head, with five on my chest. If you count two little fuzzy ones, which I do.

He frowned. "It sounded like the noise came from the garage. Let's check it out."

"Should we call Sheriff Werkle?" Mom asked.

"Only if you hear gunshots," he told her.

She rolled her eyeballs at his dumb joke. In our town, it's news if someone gets a ticket for jaywalking.

I followed Dad. He stopped in the kitchen to get a flashlight. We both stopped on the back porch to put on shoes. It was hot outside. Because it was dark, I didn't worry about the neighbors seeing me in my boxers and T-shirt.

We went to the garage.

Dad shone his flashlight at the back of the garage. He was right. The sound of breaking glass had come from there. The window beside the door was smashed.

"Strange," he said.

"The door is open," I said. "Like someone broke the glass to unlock the door."

"Why would someone do that?" he said. "What's there to steal?"

We walked closer. I was a little afraid. *Was someone still inside?*

Dad pushed the garage door open. It creaked. He looked inside, shining the flashlight ahead.

Suddenly he jumped back from the garage and screamed!

When he landed, he pointed the flashlight at his face and made monster shadows.

"Did I scare you?" he asked.

"Very funny," I said. I let go of his arm. I pretended I hadn't grabbed it in the first place. "You should listen to Mom when she tells you to grow up."

Dad grinned. "Notice she still loves me?"

"Poor woman," I said, grinning back. "Let's look inside."

I stepped past him into the garage. I flicked on the light. His car was still there. None of the tool boxes had been opened. All the garden tools were still hanging in place. It didn't look like anything had been moved or taken.

"I don't understand this," he said. "The only thing worth taking is your mountain bike. And it's still there."

"Still there?" I repeated, not sure what he meant.

Yesterday, when the bike had been stolen, I hadn't said anything to Mom and Dad. They probably wouldn't notice it was missing unless I mentioned it. I was keeping the melon-headed guy's bike at Tommy's house. I didn't want Mom and Dad to ask questions about it.

Normally, I don't hide things from them. This time though I didn't want them to worry. And I wanted all that money to be a great surprise for them.

"Of course your bike is still there," Dad said. "Why do you sound surprised?"

He pointed past his car at my twenty-one-speed Exotec-4 mountain bike. The one I'd saved a year to buy. The one that had been stolen by a melon head. The one I couldn't believe I was seeing. It was leaning against the far wall of the garage.

"I don't suppose this is the time to bring it up," he said, "but haven't I asked you to make sure you hang your bike up on the rack we built for it? I'd hate to run it over. I know how much that bike means to you."

"Yes, Dad," I said. Dad and I had spent a couple of hours one Saturday building the rack.

He patted my shoulder. "Good thing the bike is still here, isn't it. Can you imagine how you would feel if someone stole it?"

"Yeah," I said. "Just terrible."

So now that it had been returned, why didn't I feel much better?

Chapter Eleven

The next day was Saturday. There was something I wanted to find out. Ever since my bike had been stolen, I had wondered about Devil's Leap. How had the melon-headed guy managed to disappear? And where had he been going?

I wanted to ride that path to see if there were any turnoffs I couldn't remember. If I found out where he had gone, maybe I could answer some other questions. Like who did the money belong to? Why had he shot at me? Why had he returned my bike?

I wasn't going to be stupid, though. I got

on my bike and took a dozen different short-cuts to get out of town. There was no way anyone could have followed me.

It felt good to be on my own bike again. But my rear still hurt from falling the day before. And the scabs on my shin were still bright red from where the chain had scraped me. I had been hurt plenty worse before, and I was ready for some serious biking.

Even though I knew I hadn't been followed out of town, I stuck to dirt roads. It was a longer way, but it also meant no one would find me. I couldn't wait to get in some heavy-duty trail riding. I figured that once I was up in the hills, I would be completely safe.

Or so I thought.

After a half hour of riding, I was deep in the trails. I hadn't seen any other bikers. I was breathing hard, sweating hard, and loving the sun on my back. I was also halfway up the trail toward Devil's Leap. That's when I heard the sound of a helicopter.

I didn't think much about it. But then the sound got louder and louder. I looked around but didn't see it.

Two minutes later, the sound was so loud I felt it in my bones. I still couldn't see it.

Without warning, it rose from behind a ridge ahead of me. It was barely higher than the rooftop level of a house. It was so low that it spread dust and dirt in all directions below it. And it was heading straight toward me!

Chapter Twelve

I didn't think the people inside the helicopter were lost and looking to ask for directions. I turned my bike around and busted straight down the hill.

I moved fast, but the helicopter moved faster.

The helicopter passed over me. The air felt like a giant hand pushing me down. I choked on dust. The sound was like being in a tunnel with a freight train.

I slammed on my brakes and turned uphill. I was hoping I might find a place to turn off and hide. Dumb hope. As soon as I moved out of the dust, they saw me.

The helicopter banked and circled toward me.

It caught me again.

I spun a wheelie back down the hill and made another run for it.

"STOP OR WE WILL SHOOT!"

The words came from a megaphone. It reminded me of S.W.A.T. teams you sometimes see in movies. Only this wasn't a movie. And these guys weren't a S.W.A.T. team.

"STOP OR WE WILL SHOOT!"

I stopped. My Exotec-4 was nearly the best bike you could buy for these trails. But it didn't compare to a helicopter. There was no way I could outrun these guys.

I waited.

The helicopter got closer and closer to the ground. It was far enough away from me that the dust didn't blind me.

The helicopter slowly kept dropping. The hill was too steep to give it a place to land. I wondered what they would do next. Then I saw a ladder drop from the helicopter. A man climbed down. As soon as he stepped on the ground, he waved the helicopter away.

The man began to walk toward me. I thought of trying to outrun him, but the helicopter hadn't gone far. It hung in the air like a wolf waiting to pounce. If I tried anything, it could chase me in a flash.

He got close enough to shout above the noise of the helicopter.

"The guy who shot at you yesterday was just trying to get your attention. He wanted to shoot your bike tire so he could have a talk with you. If we really wanted you dead, kid, it would have happened already. Understand?"

I was scared. That's what I understood. Getting chased by a helicopter is serious business. I remembered what I had thought the day when Tommy and I had the backpack of money. *People have died for a lot less than a million dollars.*

He came closer. He was wearing a dark blue suit. He had short black hair, greased back. He had a gun in his hand. He pointed it toward me and stepped even closer.

I froze. I expected a bullet to rip my heart out.

He waved the gun. That's when I saw it was not a gun. It was a cellular phone.

"We are going to have a short discussion," he shouted. He kept waving the phone. "Then I'm going to call for my ride to pick me up again."

All I could do was nod yes. I mean, did I have a choice?

"We know you took some money," he told me. "And we want it back."

His eyes glittered. Like a snake.

"All the money is with the sheriff," I said. "If it's yours, you can get it back from him."

The man grabbed the front of my shirt. He pulled my face right up to his. I smelled cologne. Odd that I would notice cologne at a time like this.

"You're not hearing me," he said. "Fifty thousand dollars is missing. We want it back."

Fifty thousand dollars? Missing?

"You've got until three o'clock tomorrow afternoon," he yelled in my face. "Meet me right here. You bring all the money with you. All of it, down to the last hundred-dollar bill. If you don't, you're dead."

"But—"

"Shut your mouth, kid. Listen and save your life. We found you this time. We'll find you again. You can't get away. Bring us the money, and you'll be fine. So will your mom and dad."

He let go of my shirt. He patted my face like I was a little baby. I didn't like the snake smile on his face.

"If you don't bring us the money," he said. "They'll have to die too."

Another snake smile. "And by the way, I wouldn't tell them about this if I were you."

He spun around and walked away before I could say another word. A minute later, the helicopter swooped down and dropped the ladder for him. He climbed up without looking back.

The helicopter rose into the sky and soon became a black dot.

The desert hills were as quiet as they had been ten minutes earlier. It didn't seem real. But a man in a helicopter had dropped out of the sky and threatened to kill me and my parents. If I had the missing $50,000, I would have gladly given it back.

There was one slight problem. I didn't have the missing $50,000. All the money in the world that I had was a bank account of $500, money I was saving for college. Since I didn't have the missing $50,000, that left me $49,500 short.

Where was I going to get all that money by tomorrow morning?

Chapter Thirteen

After the helicopter left, I found a boulder. I sat on it and stared at the browns and reds of the desert hills. But I wasn't really looking at anything. I spent maybe a half hour thinking about what had happened in the last few days.

When I was ready to leave, I didn't go to Devil's Leap. I didn't go home. Instead, I rode to Tommy's house. I found him in his basement, lifting weights.

"Hey," he said. He was on his back on a bench, doing chest presses. Sweat dripped from his forehead.

"I'm mad at you," I said.

"Huh?"

"Because of you, I've been shot at. I've been chased by a helicopter. And my life may be over by tomorrow night."

He couldn't look me in the eyes. That's when I knew my guess was right.

"When did you take the money?" I asked. "When you first opened the backpack."

"What do you mean?" he asked, still on his back. The barbell rested on the stand above him.

"Don't make it worse by lying to me now," I said. "If you want us to stay friends, if you want me to trust you ever again, you'd better start telling the truth."

He sat up. "I'm sorry, Blake. I didn't think anything would go wrong."

"Fifty thousand dollars," I said. "Five bundles of hundred-dollar bills."

"Okay," he said. "When you were looking down Devil's Leap, I dropped the bundles down the back of my shirt. Later, when you were riding ahead of me, I moved the money into my hip pack."

"Why?"

"I couldn't help myself. All that money,

just sitting there. It was in my shirt before I knew I was doing it."

I didn't want to ask the next question. But I had to know.

"You told me to keep your name out of it at the police station," I said. "Was that so I could take the blame for the missing money?"

"No." There was hurt in his voice. "No. I didn't think anyone would even notice the money was gone. I didn't expect you would get in trouble."

He got up and walked past me. "Follow me," he said.

He stepped into his bedroom down the hall. I followed and watched him from the doorway. He reached under his mattress and pulled out two big envelopes.

One had my name on it. He handed it to me. I opened it. I saw hundred-dollar bills.

"Half of it," he said. "I wasn't going to spend any until I knew it was safe. Then I was going to give half to you. I figured later, once it was safe to keep the money, you would be happy I had set it aside."

I was staring at him.

"You've got to believe me," he said.

"We're best friends. I want it to stay that way."

I kept staring at him.

"Oh man," he said. He buried his face in his hands. "I'm sorry, Blake."

"What did you say?"

"I said I'm sorry."

"No," I said. "I mean before that. About not spending the money. You mean you haven't spent a single hundred-dollar bill?"

"You can count the money in my envelope," he said. "You'll find all $25,000."

"Impossible," I said.

"Count it!"

"I believe it's there," I said. "But now I don't know what to think."

"About us being friends?"

"Quit worrying about that," I told Tommy. I guess I didn't blame him too much for what he'd done. He'd kept half for me. He hadn't lied when it mattered. "We'll always be buds. I need you around."

"Yeah?"

"Yeah. You're uglier and dumber than I am. When you're around me, I look good."

"Hah, hah," he said. But he was smiling.

"What I can't figure out," I said. "Is how

they knew the money was missing. I thought they knew because someone in town had seen you spending it. Maybe they figured I gave it to you. But if you didn't spend any, how could they know it was missing in the first place?"

"They?"

I told him more about the helicopter and what the man in the suit had told me.

Tommy pushed his envelope in my hands. I was thinking hard, and I wasn't watching. The envelope spilled some money onto the floor.

"Well," he said, picking up a handful of hundreds. "You've got the fifty thousand dollars he asked for. You can give it back and everything will be okay."

"That is a relief," I said.

"Hey!" Tommy was looking at the bills in his hand. He was frowning.

"What?" I asked.

Tommy held out the hundred-dollar bills.

"Take a close look," he said. "Check out the serial numbers."

A couple seconds later, I understood. "All the numbers are the same," I said. "Each bill has the exact same number on it."

"Wow," Tommy said. "This money is fake."

Chapter Fourteen

Early Sunday afternoon I left the house on my mountain bike. I headed back into the hills. I had my helmet, my water bottle, and a hip pack filled with hundred-dollar bills.

I rode back up to where the guy in the suit had dropped from a helicopter. That was where he had told me to wait with the money.

I kept riding. I had other plans.

I rode higher and higher until I reached the place where the melon-headed guy had stolen my bike. From there, I rode a little farther. I found the bike trail that led to

Devil's Leap. I followed that trail right to Devil's Leap.

The trail there opened to a flat area at the edge of Devil's Leap. There was enough room for a helicopter to land.

I set my bike down and waited. I wasn't worried about not being in the right place. I knew they would find me.

Sure enough, just after 3:00, I heard the helicopter. A few minutes later, it appeared in the sky above me.

I waved at the pilot.

He brought it in closer. I could see the pilot was Melonhead. He set the helicopter down. Tiny pebbles sprayed my face from the wind the chopper raised. He shut the engine off and the blades finally stopped spinning. The silence seemed loud after all the roaring of the helicopter.

The guy in the blue suit stepped down. Today he was wearing a brown suit. And today he had a pistol in his hand, not a cellular phone.

"What do you think you're doing, kid? We told you to meet us at yesterday's place."

"You said you could find me anywhere," I told him. "And look, you did. Was it the transmitter you put under the seat of my bike?"

"You think you're smart, don't you."

"Why else would you make sure I got my bike back?" I said. "How else could you have found me yesterday?"

"Cut the talk. Do you have the money?"

I reached into my hip pack and pulled out some bills. "I've got some of it."

"That's not good news for you," he said. "I want all of it."

"Why?" I asked. "Are you afraid that someone will find out you have been counterfeiting money?"

He lifted his pistol and pointed it at my head. "Again, you're trying to show you're smart? That was the dumbest thing you could have said. Now I'll have to kill you."

"Because if anyone finds out, you'll have to stop making it, right?"

"Right. Get ready to die."

"What if I already told someone about the money?" I asked. "What if that person has some of the bills and will take them to the sheriff if I don't return from here?"

"Get on your knees, kid. I'm going to give you thirty seconds. That's time enough

63

to pray, if you want. Then I'm going to pull the trigger."

"Don't you want to know who I told?" I needed to stall for time. "Don't you want to talk about—"

"On your knees or I'll kill you *now*." His eyes were deadly. I knew he meant it.

In my plans I had thought I would be able to talk a lot longer.

I got down on my knees. What if he decided to pull the trigger immediately? As I knelt, I felt sure this was it.

He walked up to me and put the barrel of the gun against my head. It scared me so bad I wanted to cry. Dying is for old people. Kids aren't supposed to die.

I counted ten seconds. Then twenty. When was help going to arrive? Then, finally, I heard the sweet sound of Sheriff Werkle's voice.

"Drop the gun," he said to the guy in the brown suit. "If you pull the trigger, you're dead."

To me, Sheriff Werkle said, "Blake, you can stand up now."

I stood. Stretching had never felt this good. The sunshine had never seemed so bright.

Air in my lungs had never tasted so good. I was alive.

I looked at both of them. Sheriff Werkle held a shotgun in his hand. He stood beside a big boulder. The boulder was between him and the helicopter. The melon-headed guy couldn't see Sheriff Werkle. Even if he had a rifle, he couldn't do anything to him.

That was how Sheriff Werkle and I had planned it the day before. We had come out here and looked for a spot where the helicopter could land. We had picked a spot for me to wait. Sheriff Werkle would have a clear shot at whoever came to get the money. We had picked a spot where he would be protected from anyone inside the helicopter.

"Thank you," I said to Sheriff Werkle.

"No problem," he said. "I'm glad we caught the guy."

"Me too," I said. "Now my friend Tommy won't be afraid anymore."

"Tommy?" Sheriff Werkle said. "He's your friend with the rest of the money?"

"Yup." I looked at the guy in the brown suit. "I was keeping the rest of the money safe until Sheriff Werkle arrested you. Tommy made me swear that I wouldn't tell anyone, not even Sheriff Werkle. That's how afraid Tommy was."

"Tommy Nelson?" Sheriff Werkle said.

"Yeah," I said. "My best friend."

"That's all we needed to know," Sheriff Werkle said.

"We?"

"Me and Lucas," he answered me.

"Lucas?"

"One of my partners," Sheriff Werkle said. "The guy standing in front of you. Lucas meet Blake. Blake meet Lucas."

"Cut the funny stuff," Lucas told Werkle.

Sheriff Werkle pointed his shotgun at my stomach. "Too bad, Blake. You were smart enough to figure out the fake money, but not smart enough to figure out the rest."

"But—"

"Don't you get it? Yesterday when you told me that a friend had some of the money, I went along with this to get his name from you."

Sheriff Werkle smiled. "Now we have his name. We're going to keep you alive until we get Tommy. Once we have him and the rest of the money, you're both dead."

Chapter Fifteen

You're part of this?" I said. "But why?"

"Why?" Werkle said. "One hundred thousand dollars a week, that's why."

"Shut up," Lucas said to Sheriff Werkle. "Let's grab the kid's friend and get this over with."

"I think I have some of it figured out," I said. "The melon-headed guy who stole my bike—he was taking the money to the river, right?"

"Mexico's on the other side. Someone might notice a helicopter but never our man on his mountain bike." Sheriff Werkle told me. I noticed he held the shotgun real steady. I didn't like looking at the black hole pointing toward me.

"But why smuggle money out of the country?" I asked. "Why not spend it here?"

"Simple," Sheriff Werkle told me. "We couldn't spend it anywhere inside the United States. It wouldn't take long for someone to figure it out that phony money was hitting the banks. The FBI would start looking for us. They wouldn't catch us, but we'd have to stop spending it."

Sheriff Werkle pointed south. "We sell the fake money across the border. Once a week our bike guy makes a delivery. The Mexicans we work with only pay us 10 percent, but on a million, that's a hundred thousand dollars. From there, they take the money all over the world. In just about any country you name, American dollars are as good as gold. And in those countries, people don't know the difference between real money and a good fake."

"I see," I said. "That's why you needed to get all of the missing fifty thousand dollars back. Until now, no one in the United States knew you were making the stuff."

"And they won't ever," Werkle said. "Getting you and Tommy wraps this up. Why do you think I made sure you kept the money a secret from your parents?"

I shook my head from side to side. "What rotten luck," I said. "Bringing the backpack full of money right back to you."

"There's no luck involved. That's why I'm part of this," Sheriff Werkle told me. "I'd be the first one to hear from the FBI or anyone else if the money was ever discovered. Not only that, but I know when the customs police are making patrols."

"So you let the guy on the bike know when it's safe to make a trip with the money?"

Werkle grinned. "It's the perfect set up, isn't it? No cop would ever be able to follow him. He takes a path into the hills and back down to the river. He puts the money in a remote-controlled boat and sends it across to people waiting on the other side. After they unload it, he gets the boat back and hides it until the next delivery."

I snapped my fingers. "The remote control in the backpack! You took that too."

"Let's go," Lucas said.

"Relax," Werkle told him. "The kid should at least know why he'll die."

"It does sound perfect," I said quickly. I wanted the sheriff to keep talking. "Even if the police got the boat, the guy on the bike can make a getaway. On his bike, he can go places they can't follow."

"You think pretty good," Sheriff Werkle said.

"One thing," I said. I pointed at Devil's Leap. "How does he get across?"

"A homemade aluminum bridge," Werkle said. "It's lightweight and sturdy. He sets it from one side to the other. After he crosses, he pulls it over and hides it. On his way back, he hides it on this side again. That way, nobody can follow him any farther than Devil's Leap. It's foolproof.

"Except for the flat tire he had."

"Yes, Blake. Except for the flat tire. Any other questions before I go to get Tommy?"

"No," I said, "but do you have any questions for me?"

"Why should I?"

"Well," I said, "I knew it was you behind this."

Sheriff Werkle laughed. "Nice try, kid."

"Your brother has a printing shop. I'll bet that's where you guys make the money."

"This kid's getting on my nerves," Lucas said. "Let's shoot him now."

Werkle waved Lucas into silence. "Let the kid talk," Werkle said. "I find this interesting. Yes, we do the work in my brother's print shop. Once we decided to start making phony money, I ran for sheriff to make sure I could take care of the law in these parts. Anything else, Sherlock Holmes?"

"Besides Tommy, you were the only one in town who knew I found the backpack with money," I told Sheriff Werkle. "Besides Tommy, you were the only one who knew about the melon-headed guy. I sure hadn't told Melonhead my name. So how did he find me to return my bike?"

I shrugged. "Unless, of course, you told him."

I went on before Werkle could say anything. "There's one other thing. Tommy hasn't spent any of the money. And Lucas here told me to return fifty thousand dollars. That's the exact amount Tommy took. How could Lucas know how much was missing? Unless you told him how much I turned in."

Lucas laughed at Sheriff Werkle. "The kid's got you there. Serves you right for showing off and blabbing your mouth."

"All right then," Werkle said to me, "if you know so much, Blake, why did you fall for this trap."

"I didn't," I said. I pointed up the canyon walls behind him. "You did."

Lucas and Werkle looked where I was pointing. I dove for the boulder and kept rolling as rifle shots filled the air.

Chapter Sixteen

From behind the boulder, I listened.

"Those shots were a warning!" my dad shouted from his spot in the rocks. I grinned. Dad sounded pretty tough.

"Drop your weapons!" This was the voice of the state trooper we'd called the day before. "You in the helicopter, come out with your hands on your head."

With the helicopter shut down, there was no way Melonhead could escape. He stepped down with his hands on his head.

"There are four of us! Don't do anything

stupid!" Tommy's dad shouted. He sounded just as tough as my dad.

"Hit the ground, scumballs!" This was from Tommy. "Eat dirt!"

When I heard Tommy, I decided there should be a law against watching too many Sylvester Stallone movies.

"Blake!" Dad shouted. "Take their weapons and stay well clear of them."

I got to my feet. Sheriff Werkle, Lucas, and Melonhead stood beside each other. Their hands were high. Their guns were on the ground.

I picked up the sheriff's shotgun and Lucas's pistol and stepped back. I watched the state trooper climb down from his hiding spot. He had a grim smile on his wide face. My dad, Tommy's dad, and Tommy followed him down.

"Kids are stupid, huh, sheriff?" Lucas said to Werkle. "It will be like stealing candy from a baby, huh?"

Lucas spit on the ground in disgust. "Werkle, you'd better hope you don't end up near my jail cell."

My dad joined me as the state trooper handcuffed the prisoners.

Tommy and his dad stood together nearby, keeping their rifles pointed and ready. Tommy's dad was a little shorter than Tommy and a lot wider. I wouldn't want to mess with either of them.

"Good to see you folks," Sheriff Werkle said. "I was just trying to arrest these guys, and it got a little out of control."

"Nice try, Werkle," Dad said. "We know you're up to your neck in this one. Why do you think we came in earlier to set up this trap?"

"You can't prove I had anything to do with it," Werkle said. "So I suggest you let me arrest these two men and—"

Werkle stopped talking. He watched me pull a small tape recorder from my hip pack.

"You guys had remote-control boats and tracking transmitters," I said, holding up the tape recorder. "The best I could do was this. I hope it's enough."

I pressed rewind on the tape recorder, stopped it a few seconds later and began to play the tape back. Sheriff Werkle's voice came out very clear: *Yes, we do the work in my brother's print shop. Once we decided to start making phony money, I ran for sheriff to make sure I could take care of the law in these parts. Anything else, Sherlock Holmes?*

"Busted," Tommy told Werkle. "You're big-time busted."

Tommy looked at me. I looked at him. We high-fived each other.

"Dad," I said, "I think I've done everything I can do here. Would it be okay if Tommy and I hit some major trails? "

I lifted my bike as I talked. "After all, the Summit Race is coming up. I'd hate to let a little thing like this get in the way of practice."

And Now, a Word from the Author ...

Dear Reader:

No one likes to think about dying. In fact, we live in a society that tries to make death invisible. Dying people are hidden in hospitals. Fancy funeral homes make bodies look as life-like as possible. If we even talk about dying, someone will usually frown and tell us to change the subject.

Death often seems very far away—almost unreal. A summer can seem to last forever. How can we imagine what it's like to be eighty years old and facing death?

There are more pleasant things to think

about. Mountain bike riding. Baseball games on hot days. Hanging out with friends.

But if you've ever talked to people who have come close to dying, you've likely heard how much more precious life has become. Because life was nearly taken from them, they realize what a gift life is. They want to enjoy every single day they have.

In *Cliff Dive*, Blake Coffey is suddenly faced with the possibility that he will die. When the trigger is not pulled, when his life is given back to him, he tells you how much brighter the sunshine seems, how good the air in his lungs feels.

(Try something right now. Hold your breath for a moment. Imagine you can't take another breath. You'll discover how much something as simple as breathing means to you. To be alive is a wonderful thing.)

More important, there is another reason to stop once in a while and think about dying. We have to ask ourselves what happens after our life on earth.

I feel sorry for people who don't understand that life is a gift from God. They don't understand that when life on earth ends, the soul continues forever. How sad and hopeless life must be for them. They think that when they die, there is nothing else. I think that is why so many people try to ignore or hide death. For them, it is bad, bad news. It is the worst thing that can happen.

When we have faith that God is behind everything, we have hope. When we know that He created this world and sent His Son as a way for us to reach Him, death is not the end. Instead, death is like stepping through a curtain to meet Someone who loves us and has been waiting for us.

I ended this story where it needed to end as a story, with the bad guys captured. I know, however, that if Blake's story continued after the showdown, we would see him asking questions about faith and why it is important in life. After all, he discovered something that is easy to forget when you are young—life on this earth is not forever.

Wondering what that means, and deciding what you will do about it is the most important decision you can make.

From your friend,

Sigmund Brouwer

Read and collect all of
Sigmund Brouwer's

S E R I E S™

Turn the page for an exciting preview of

SNOWBOARDING
. . . to the Extreme:

Rippin'

Keegan Bishop is one of the hottest skiers on the hill. Now he wants to try snowboarding. But weird things are happening to kids who hang out and go rippin'—weird enough that Keegan's about to go on the ride of his life.

Go!" My coach yelled.

I went.

I blinked twice. The wind filled my lungs. It filled my ears like the roar of a freight train.

I cut left to miss an ice patch. I hit a jump at freeway speed. I flew into the air at least one story off the ground. I leaned forward and made sure my skis stayed straight.

I thumped back to earth and began to

crouch to block less wind. At this speed, the trees on the sides of the run flashed by like fence boards.

Halfway down I knew I was skiing the best I ever had. If I kept pushing, I would easily stay number one.

Beneath my helmet, I grinned.

And as I cut into a steep turn, I saw it. But I couldn't believe it.

Wire. Black cable wire. Stretched between two trees. Waist high. With me screaming toward it at 102 feet per second. Hitting the wire at that speed would cut me in two.

I dropped my poles and sat on my skis. Balancing at seventy miles per hour on two thin pieces of plastic and metal, this was not as easy as sitting down for dinner. But I had no choice.

The wire scraped the top of my helmet as I slid beneath it. I wobbled. To keep my balance, I slapped my hand on the snow. My hand bounced off. The force nearly knocked me over the other way. I fought to stay on my skis for another hundred yards.

Finally, I was able to turn and dig the edges of my skis into the snow. I began to slow down.

But just when I thought I was safe, I hit a patch of ice. My skis slid out from under me. I began to tumble and roll down the hill. The sky tilted around me. The snow seemed to spin. The trees rose and fell at crazy angles. I felt like a cannonball bouncing down a set of stairs. Both of my skis popped loose as I rolled down the hill.

The best thing to do in a fall is also the hardest thing to do. You have to go limp like a rag doll. If you stay tight, you can rip your muscles and snap your bones.

I waited to stop tumbling. I finally fell into some deep, soft snow at the edge of the trees. I came to a stop with a *whump*!

I tasted for blood. Sometimes when you fall you bite your tongue. No blood.

I blinked. At least my eyelids worked.

I wiggled my fingers. They worked too.

So did my arms. And my legs.

That was a good sign. If I could move all my body parts, I knew I hadn't broken my back.

I thought about Garth. His accident happened two weeks ago. He was still in a hospital. Eating Jell-O. Drinking warm milk. Being bossed around by big, ugly nurses.

I took off my helmet and shook my hair loose.

Then I had another thought I didn't want to think. Black wire stretched between two trees is not an accident. What if the same thing had happened to Garth?

If Garth's broken legs weren't an accident, there were other questions I didn't want to ask.

Who was doing this? And why?

**For more exciting sports stories
don't miss**

SIGMUND BROUWER'S

SERIES

Each book weaves a tantalizing
sports mystery that includes plenty
of on-ice hockey drama.

Rebel Glory

B. T. McPhee, the star defenseman of the Red Deer Rebels, likes his chances of making it as a pro. But he doesn't like the small "accidents" that may keep his team from making the playoffs—and keep him off the team. Unless he can unravel the mystery, the team's season—and his own career—will surely end. (ISBN 0-8499-3637-3)

All-Star Pride

Hog Burnell is playing on a WHL All-Star Team touring Russia. The goal is to beat the Russian All-Stars in the best-of-seven series to be shown as a television special. But it doesn't take Hog long to discover there's plenty money to be made along the way . . . if he's willing to pay the price for it. (ISBN 0-8499-3638-1)

Thunderbird Spirit

Dakota Smith plays for the Seattle Thunderbirds. Unfortunately, there are more than a few unwilling to accept a Native American in hockey. For Mike "Crazy" Keats, haunted by a troubled background that fast makes him friends with Dakota, it means hockey just got more complicated. (ISBN 0-8499-3639-X)

Winter Hawk Star

Riley Judd is a star center for the Portland Winter Hawks. When he and teammate Tyler Watson are given the choice of working with street kids or getting kicked off the team, they take what they think is the easy way out. But they soon discover that it could cost their lives to give the kids the help they really need.
(ISBN 0-8499-3640-3)

Blazer Drive

Josh Elroy, a left winger for the Kamloops Blazers, finds more than a dozen dead cattle on his dad's ranch. With playoffs ahead, Josh is afraid of what will happen if he gets too involved with the ranch business. But as he learns more, he's afraid of what will happen if he doesn't.

(0-8499-3983-6; available 12/96)